Vivian French   Joanne Par

Bubble
Trouble

MACMILLAN CHILDREN'S BOOKS

The Shiny Button Café opened at ten o'clock on Mondays, and Ellie, Emma and their mums were the first inside. The two mums ordered coffee, and sat down to chat.

As soon as they were settled, Ellie pulled at Emma's sleeve. "They're busy," she whispered. "Let's see if Sparkle Street is waiting for us!"

But Emma was already staring at the mirror
at the back of the shop. "Look!" she pointed.
"I can see Fairy Pink . . . and she's FLYING!"

The two girls ran to the mirror, and
scrambled through as fast as they could.

As Emma and Ellie climbed through the mirror
and into Fairy Pink's pretty hotel hallway, Fairy
Pink waved from up near the ceiling.

"I'm SO glad you're here!" she called.
"I've dropped my wand and I can't get down."
Emma looked at her in surprise. "Why can't
you fly down?" she asked. "You've got wings!"

Fairy Pink nodded. "Yes, but I made
a twinkly-pink hurrying-scurrying
spell and it went a little bit wrong."

Ellie climbed onto the table and handed
Fairy Pink the wand.
"Pinkly twinkly!" Fairy Pink waved the wand and
flew down to the ground. "Thank you so much!"
"Why were you making a hurrying-scurrying
spell?" Emma asked.

The fairy sighed. "I wanted everything to be spingly spangly sparkly clean. The hotel inspector is coming today, and I thought a spell would save time but now I'll never be ready."

"We'll help you," Ellie said.
"We're good at helping!" Emma agreed.
"We'll start in the laundry room," Fairy Pink decided. "There are lots of sheets and towels to wash."

Ellie picked up a box of washing powder, but Fairy Pink waved her wand. "I'll make a spell," she said.

"Scrub-a-dub-dubbitty!"

The washing machines began to spin. Faster and faster and FASTER they went.

"Oops!" Fairy Pink waved her wand again. Bubbles floated into the air . . . more and more and MORE bubbles.

"Quick!" Ellie said. "Open the door!"
As Emma opened the back door Posy Pink,
Dominic Domino and Hannah McSpanner
came hurrying up the path.

"Hello," said Posy. "What a lot of bubbles!"
Emma told her what had happened, and Posy
began to giggle. "Grandma's HOPELESS at
spells. She always gets them wrong!"

Posy rushed up to Fairy Pink.
"No more spells, Grandma!"
Fairy Pink looked sad. "Not even
a tiny one to tidy the bedrooms?"

"No," Posy said firmly, putting the wand in
her pocket. Hannah waved her spanner.
"I'll see what I can do with those machines!"
"And I'll pop the bubbles," said Dominic
Domino. "Fairy Pink, you can help me."

Posy laughed. "And we'll tidy the bedrooms."
As soon as they got upstairs Posy pulled out the wand,
her eyes shining. "Tinkly pinkly twinkly!" she said.

42 43 44

Emma stared at Ellie. Ellie stared at Emma.
"We've got WINGS!" they shouted.
"We'll be finished in no time now," Posy said.

Emma, Ellie and Posy flew
round the bedrooms . . .
and they tidied and dusted
and polished.

They flew round the bathrooms . . .
and they dusted and polished
and tidied.

They flew down the stairs
to the dining room . . .
and they polished and
tidied and dusted.

And last of all they flew back to the
laundry room, where Fairy Pink was
popping the very last bubble.
"It's all spingly spangly sparkly clean
for the hotel inspector!" said Ellie.

P'RRRRRING!

went the bell on
the front desk.

"That'll be him now!" said Posy.
Fairy Pink looked nervous. "I'd better
show him round."
"Do you think it'll be all right?" Emma
whispered as Fairy Pink hurried away.
Ellie rubbed her nose. "I do hope so."

When they came back the inspector was smiling. "Congratulations!" he said. "What spingly spangly sparkly clean rooms! I hereby award you ten silver stars for your fairy hotel!"

Fairy Pink pointed to Ellie, Emma and Posy. "These are the REAL stars," she said. "I couldn't have done it without them."

"Well then," said the inspector, "they deserve
an award too!" He opened his case and out flew
hundreds and hundreds of shiny stars, filling
the room with sparkles.

"Oh dear," he said. "That always happens."
"I'll make a spell to put them back in your case," Fairy Pink
told him, but then she paused. "No. Posy dear, could you do it?"
Ellie and Emma smiled and smiled as Posy waved the wand . . .

. . . and the stars flew back. Just three were left, one each for Posy, Emma and Ellie. "THANK YOU!" Emma and Ellie said together, and then . . .

Cuckoo! Cuckoo!

"What's that?" asked Hannah McSpanner.
"It's the cuckoo," Ellie told her. "We've got to go."
"That's so sad," said Dominic Domino. "I was
hoping you'd come and see my toy shop."

"We'll come next Monday," Emma promised,
and then she and Ellie flew through the mirror . . .

. . . and arrived on the other side with a bump.
"Goodness!" said Ellie's mum. "Just look at the time!"
"Time flies when you're having fun," said Emma's mum.

Ellie looked at Emma and smiled.
"It's not just time that flies, is it?"
Emma began to giggle. "No! We flew too!"

"I LOVE Sparkle Street," Ellie said as she
buttoned up her coat.
"Hurrah for Mondays!" Emma agreed, and she
took Ellie's hand as they hurried out of the café.

First published 2011 by Macmillan Children's Books
a division of Macmillan Publishers Limited
20 New Wharf Road, London N1 9RR
Basingstoke and Oxford
Associated companies throughout the world
www.panmacmillan.com

ISBN: 978-0-230-70956-0

1 3 5 7 9 8 6 4 2

A CIP catalogue record for this book is available from the British Library.

Printed in China